DEEP-SEA DASH

BY KNIFE & PACKER

Kane Miller
A DIVISION OF EDC PUBLISHING

First American Edition 2016
Kane Miller, A Division of EDC Publishing

Text and illustrations copyright © Knife and Packer 2015
First published by Scholastic Australia, a division of Scholastic Australia Pty Limited in 2015.
This edition published under license from Scholastic Australia Pty Limited.

For information contact:
Kane Miller, A Division of EDC Publishing
P.O. Box 470663
Tulsa, OK 74147-0663
www.kanemiller.com
www.edcpub.com
www.usbornebooksandmore.com

Library of Congress Control Number: 2015938804

Manufactured by Regent Publishing Services, Hong Kong
Printed December 2015 in ShenZhen, Guangdong, China

Paperback ISBN: 978-1-61067-398-3
Hardcover ISBN: 978-1-61067-478-2

DEEP-SEA DASH

The road ahead is dangerous! Can you handle:

Hairy scary polar bears?!
Super-toothy sharks?!
Grabbing squid?!

If not, then turn back now!
If you can, then hold on
tight and good luck!

MEET THE WHEELNUTS!

Rust Bucket 3000

UPGRADE! 9 fishy fishing rod

The Rust Bucket 3000 is the most high-tech robot car in the universe. Driven by super-sophisticated robots Nuts and Boltz, this team is always happy to use robo-gadgets to get ahead of the opposition.

The Wheel Deal

Dustin Grinner and Myley Twinkles aren't just car drivers, they are actually super-cheesy pop singers and stars of daytime TV. The Wheel Deal, their super-souped-up stretch limo, is showbiz on wheels!

UPGRADE! 3 waterproof speaker

Dino-Wagon

This prehistoric car is driven by the Dino-Crew—Turbo Rex and Flappy, a pterodactyl and all-around nervous passenger. Powered by an active volcano, this vehicle has a turbo boost unlike anything seen on Earth!

UPGRADE! 5 extra-thick skin

The Flying Diaper
Babies are great, but they are also gross, and nothing could be more gross than this pair. Gurgle

The Supersonic Sparkler
Petrolnella and Dieselina (known as Nelly and Dee-Dee) are fairies with attitude, and with a sprinkling of fairy dust, the Supersonic Sparkler has a surprising turn of speed.

UPGRADE!
8
Super powder splatterer

The Jumping Jalopy
This grandfather and grandson team drive a not-always-reliable 1930s Bugazzi. Although determined to win on skill alone, they are not above some "old-school cunning" to keep in the race.

UPGRADE!
11
superfast propeller

CHAPTER 1

An icy wind howled, snowflakes swirled and frost settled on the cars. But multibillionaire race organizer Warren "Wheelie" Wheelnut's fourth race wasn't taking place on the snow and ice of the Arctic. As soon as Wheelie appeared, it was obvious where this race was happening because Warren was wearing a shiny new wet suit, snorkel and mask. This race was taking place *under* the snow and ice of the Arctic—UNDERWATER!

"A warm welcome to the f-f-f-freezing Arctic,"
said the shivering billionaire. "As you can see, this
is extreme, unwelcoming and downright
like my races to be.

adjusted his diving mask.

"The rules are simple—there *are no* rules! Now
let me introduce you to the Wheelnuts themselves
and their 'submersi-cars!'"

Wheelie asked each team what they thought of racing underwater.

"First up, the Flying Diaper!"

It feels a bit like bath time ...

As long as there's no hair washing, we'll be fine!

"Next, the Wheel Deal!"

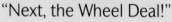

We're never going to be WASHED UP!

We'll be making a BIG splash!

"So, how does the Dino-Wagon feel about going underwater?"

Well, dinosaurs started life underwater, so it's a bit like going home!

"Next, we have the Supersonic Sparkler!"

We plan to twinkle in the sparkly Arctic Ocean!

It's going to be fun, like a trip to the fish-and-chip shop!

"Finally, we have the Rust Bucket 3000!"

Our car has been coated in rust-proof paint!

So there we have it, ladies and gentleman. Please give a round of applause that's as big as an ocean for the Wheelnuts!

"But don't for one second think this race is just about the freezing cold waters of the Arctic. *That's* just for starters!" chuckled Wheelie. "The race will take them to every corner of the sea from cold to hot, with challenges of every shape and size—many with fins and most with sharp teeth!

"Now before they hit the drink, let me tell you all how the scoring works. There are trophies for the top three drivers, plus Wheelnut Gold Stars to be won at checkpoints and in the world-famous Wheelnut Challenge," he continued. "And Gold Stars can be used at the Wheelnut Garage for car upgrades and cheats!

"Enough with the talk, it's time to get wet!" said Wheelie as he moved into position next to a large ship's bell, ready to start the race.

the crowd went wild … for the first time ever the Wheelnuts were underwater!

Nothing could have prepared the Wheelnuts for the sensation of driving underwater. The Flying Diaper was going at an amazing speed—but unfortunately it was upside down and heading in the wrong direction!

"This feels really weird," said Gurgle.

"My head's tickling," said Burp.

The Jumping Jalopy was having trouble with its rudder. It was going really fast—in a circle!

"I thought I'd feel seasick, not dizzy!" wailed James.

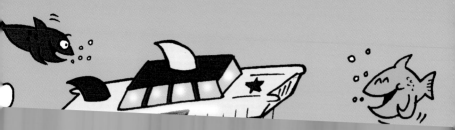

The Rust Bucket 3000 had engine troubles and was sinking like a stone.

"Is it me or is it getting dark down here?" asked Boltz as Nutz tried to kick-start the engine.

But the Wheel Deal was having the opposite problem—it *couldn't* sink!

"I've never been so keen to hit rock bottom!" wailed Myley.

The two cars to get the hang of the environment first and get into the lead were the Dino-Wagon and the Supersonic Sparkler, with the Dino crew edging ahead ...

But as they vied for position something in the icy waters started to circle them.

"I think we may be about to encounter the local wildlife," said Flappy.

And as the Supersonic Sparkler made its move to overtake the Dino-Wagon, it too became aware of dark shadows …

"I don't *mind* shadows," said Dee-Dee. "But that one has beady eyes and it's heading straight for us!"

CHAPTER 2

...tures stirring in

frighteningly large A... ...
taking far too much interest in the race.

One by one the cars picked up speed—the race
was well and truly on! The Rust Bucket 3000 team
kick-started their engine and were off the bottom,
the Jumping Jalopy had straightened its rudder and
even the Wheel Deal was finally submerged.

But as they tried to overtake each other, one of the cars felt itself rise in the water.

"OK, Boltz, you can turn the upward thruster off now," said Nutz. "We're at the right level to race …"

But no matter how many times Boltz hit the OFF switch, they just kept on rising and rising.

They weren't the only car that was rising up through the water. The Jumping Jalopy and the Wheel Deal were also on their way up—and they were all being pushed there by huge hairy creatures!

"This is sooo off script!" wailed Dustin. "If we wanted to 'head to the top,' we'd release a hit single, you furry menaces!"

"Walruses, said Campbell, "one of the world's largest mammals … but that's not all!" In fact, every single one of the Wheelnuts were under attack. "The Dino-Wagon is being prodded by a large narwhal and the Supersonic Sparkler is being tossed around by seals …"

BOINK!

The drivers were getting *really* worried. Although they had powerful engines, they were no match for these enormous Arctic Sea dwellers.

"What do they want?" shouted James as the Jumping Jalopy was tossed clean out of the water.

"Let me see," said Campbell, stroking his moustache. He could be strangely calm in the most frightening circumstances. "They live on fish, so they don't want to eat us. And they can see we are passing through, so we are not invading their territory … wait a second—I've got it! Do you have your soccer ball with you?"

Campbell grabbed James' soccer ball and shouted out to the assorted sea mammals. "So you want to have some fun? Great! Play with this!" He ̶ ̶ ̶ to open the car's protective dome

The cars all sank back under the water—and the race was able to resume!

"Just as I suspected, they only wanted to play!" exclaimed Campbell. "I'll get you a new ball when we finish the race."

CHAPTER 3

But one car was so far off course it had missed all the trouble with the wildlife. It had taken the Flying Diaper crew some time to work out their problem, but they were finally the right way up. They were also in last position. And when a Wheelnut really wants to get boosted they forget about good driving. If they really want to get ahead in the race, they are more than happy to *cheat!*

"Time for some nautical naughtiness!" said Gurgle. "I think you'll find those used diapers we kept will work great"

Gurgle pressed a button and a large tube
appeared on the underside of their car. Gurgle and
Burp had to hold their noses—even underwater the
~~... was unbearable.~~

But before we see what happens when Burp presses FIRE, let's have a sneak peek inside the Wheelnut Garage and see some of the things you can buy there …

Oils and Lubricants

All the Wheelnuts have seriously fast engines, but these special oils and lubricants can help the cars in extreme conditions, like on the surface of the moon or underwater.

Missiles and Projectiles

One of the best ways to cheat is with one of these—with exploding diapers, expanding teddies and live dragons, there's a missile for every occasion.

Engine Power-ups

very turbo upgrade and
ngine booster available

…ould sell pets especially
for your car. From
dashboard fish to front-
seat frogs, leg-rest lions
o laughing lemurs, these
will liven up any vehicle.

Want to add some
"bite" to your
wheels? Then the
Wheelnut Garage
has every shape
and size of tire—
including some
with *teeth!*

Wheels

Burp pressed FIRE and a stinking torpedo flew out from the Flying Diaper!

The Wheel Deal swerved into an iceberg!

The Jumping Jalopy stalled and began to plummet!

The Supersonic
Sparkler's wings
began to droop …

The Rust Bucket
3000 team were
short-circuiting!

The smell is causing
an onboard computer
malfunction!

The Dino-Wagon
was suddenly blinded!

We're trapped in
a stink cloud!

Howling with laughter at the carnage the Diaper Torpedo had created, the Flying Diaper swept from last place to first!

"Ha! Ha! The torpedo has caused complete havoc!" chuckled Gurgle. "And it didn't even have to hit anyone!"

"Where is it now?" asked Burp. "I think we need to know where it is …"

The Flying Diaper crew only enjoyed their lead for a few moments. It wasn't long before they discovered *exactly* where the torpedo had finished up—and it wasn't going to be good news!

In the distance there was a loud thud and a squelching noise. The torpedo had hit something— something big and unfriendly.

"What is that swimming this way?" wailed Burp.

and turning in a bid to escape.

They could feel the polar bear's teeth clamp onto the exhaust pipe when Gurgle finally spotted a means of escape. "Over there … a forest!" he shouted.

Burp pulled on the steering wheel with all his might and the Flying Diaper swerved and darted into a thick forest of green seaweed.

"You've done it!" cried Gurgle. "We've escaped the polar bear's clutches!"

CHAPTER 4

T he Flying Diaper was not alone—all the other

The Rust Bucket 3000 was soon in the lead—they were able to use a robotic plant chopper to clear a path.

But right behind them was the Wheel Deal—Dustin was in a wet suit on top of the car, grabbing kelp and weaving it into hula dresses …

Next was the Dino-Wagon—they were feeding the kelp to a large diplodocus whose head had popped out of the volcano.

The Supersonic Sparkler was using its wings as extra propellers to dodge the seaweed.

The Flying Diaper was firing out toxic burps that was turning the kelp into vegetable soup …

In last place, the Jumping Jalopy wasn't really coping at all. In fact, the car was covered in so much of the green kelp that it looked like a giant green sea monster!

All the drivers were relieved to see the kelp thinning out, but the racecourse was now heading in an even scarier direction …

"Farther *down?*" gasped James as the Jumping Jalopy broke free of its tangling seaweed and swerved past the Supersonic Sparkler.

The Wheelnuts were about to discover that the race was going much, much deeper. As they drove on, they heard a gurgle behind them that sounded like a squeal. Something, or someone, was being chased out of the kelp …

CHAPTER 5

Two men in wet suits were swimming as fast
~~~~~~~~~~~~ would manage. Behind

beasties!" ~~~~~~

"Bad otters, back off!" wheedled the taller man.

It was none other than Wipeout Wheelnut and his unpleasant sidekick, Dipstick. Unlike his multi-billionaire brother, Wheelie, Wipeout did *not* run a successful tournament. Instead, he had made it his life's mission to ruin his brother's race and he saw the underwater course as the perfect setting.

But at that moment, wrecking the race was the last thing on his mind as he tried to evade the angry otters.

"I *told* you to park closer to the kelp!" barked Wipeout.

The two villains were now swimming towards a shipwreck. But this was no ordinary shipwreck—it was actually a submarine in disguise!

correct, I know the exact place to intercept them.

The evil villain jabbed a pin into a map.

"And when we do, we'll have a deep-sea surprise to take their breath away!" chortled Dipstick.

CHAPTER 6

Meanwhile the Wheelnuts were heading straight down—it was underwater warfare to get to the front of the pack. The Rust Bucket 3000, being so heavy, was sinking superfast, but with the Wheel Deal gaining on it, the robotic duo decided it was time to get nasty.

"Now, where is that stuff I saw rolling around in here?" said Nutz, looking under his seat. "It will be the perfect cheat …"

"You mean the Eco-Oil-Slick-In-A-Can?" said Boltz, holding up a yucky-looking container. "Harmless to the sea—but harmful to our rivals!"

Nutz placed the icky liquid in a tube and fired it out the back of the car. A large green oil slick was now hanging in the water and was causing mayhem with the other drivers.

Sparkler swerved off course.

"Get it off our windshield!" said Campbell as the Jumping Jalopy narrowly missed the Flying Diaper. As the cars tried to avoid the green slick, the Rust Bucket 3000 cruised ahead.

But one of the cars was not affected by the green slick. The Dino-Wagon was heading in the opposite direction—into even *deeper* waters

"Lucky we upgraded the car's reptile skin," said Flappy.

"It's amazing what you can buy at the Wheelnut Garage," said Turbo Rex. "But Dino-Wagon fuel is *not* on sale there."

The Dino-Wagon's rear-mounted volcano was the car's only source of power and it was fueled with molten volcanic rocks. These only had to be replaced occasionally—the only trouble was you had to go into a deep-sea volcano to find one.

The deeper they went, the darker it got, until
Flappy spotted a bright light in the distance.

"How kind—there's a streetlight to show us
the way," said Flappy. "Follow that glow." But the

After swerving, flipping and diving, the Dino-
Wagon finally got away from the anglerfish and
found a perfect volcano. It was time to lower in a
small thick-skinned dinosaur and fetch a molten
rock.

With Turbo Rex and Flappy reloading the car with volcanic rock, let's take a closer look at their car—as we put the Dino-Wagon UNDER THE SPOTLIGHT!

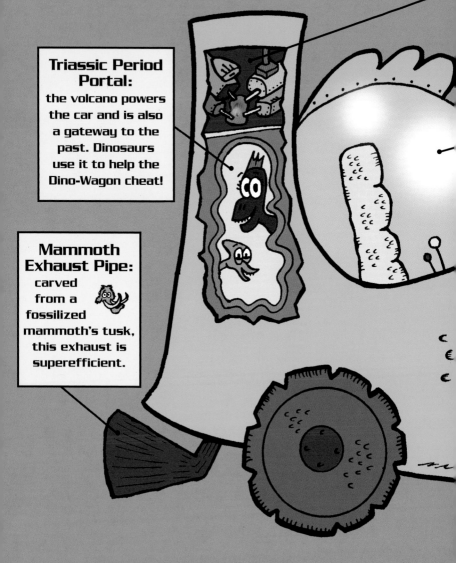

Triassic Period Portal: the volcano powers the car and is also a gateway to the past. Dinosaurs use it to help the Dino-Wagon cheat!

Mammoth Exhaust Pipe: carved from a fossilized mammoth's tusk, this exhaust is superefficient.

Volcano-powered Jet Engine: powered by red-hot volcanic rocks, this engine is superfast

temperature and pterodactyl poop! Less resistant to pterodactyl poop!

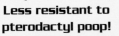

Bionic Bodywork: carved from a very rare and superlight ancient stone, it is unbreakable and heat resistant.

Wheelosaurus Tires: made from the skin of a thick-hided dinosaur that sheds its skin. Almost unbreakable with a superstrong road grip.

"Little Vulcanito just loves that heat!" exclaimed Turbo Rex as she winched up the diminutive reptile who was clinging to the perfect chunk of rock.

Turbo Rex then lowered the rock into the car's volcano. The car rumbled, spluttered then sprang forward at huge speed.

"Wahayyyyyy!!!" squealed Flappy.

"Now to rejoin the race!" said Turbo Rex as they powered back onto the course. In the distance were the rest of the Wheelnuts—and beyond them, the first checkpoint.

CHAPTER 7

The cars were all heading rapidly down, down,

"Well, we're not here to relax," said Nutz, "we're here to race and the first checkpoint is in sight!"

The other Wheelnuts had also spotted the checkpoint and with Gold Stars, not to mention prestige, at stake, the race was on!

"My ears are popping!" said Gurgle as they plummeted farther and farther down.

"Never mind your ears, Gurgle," said Burp, before shouting, "Take that, you old tin can!" as he cut in front of the Jumping Jalopy.

"Road hogs!" said Campbell, shaking his fist.

"Don't you mean 'water hogs'?" guffawed Gurgle as they took the lead.

"That's it! Time to get nasty!" said Dustin in the Wheel Deal, which was in last place. It had just been overtaken by the Dino-Wagon, which was enjoying a fresh boost of power from its new

"It's time to take these nobodies down—showbiz style," said Myley. "Oh yes! It's time to unleash … the Encore!!!"

Now, the Craziest Race on Earth is a race with no rules, but every now and then a team can unleash a cheat so nasty it's known as their "SUPER-SICK MEGA-NAUGHTY CHEAT."

SUPER-SICK MEGA-NAUGHTY CHEAT!

A huge waterproof speaker emerged from the back of the car and locked into position as two microphones flipped out of the dashboard. Dustin and Myley each picked up one, cleared their throats … then blasted out their worst-ever love song as loud as they could.

Although it sounded pretty dreadful inside the Wheel Deal—outside, where the speaker was blaring out, the effect was extraordinary. At first the seabed started to rumble and the trench walls started to shudder, but when Dustin and Myley hit the chorus, all kinds of craziness started to happen!

Deep-sea marine life was trying to block its ears and get away from the racket. The Wheel Deal cheat

The Rust Bucket 3000 was pelted by fleeing octopuses, the Jumping Jalopy was jammed under a falling piece of rock and the Flying Diaper had driven into a hole …

As the Wheel Deal flew towards the checkpoint, only the Dino-Wagon crew had survived the earsplitting attack by covering their ears with giant earmuffs—two sets of saber-toothed tiger kittens! Both cars now sped towards the line. The Dino-Wagon was in the lead, but with one final effort, Myley started … rapping! That was *too* much, and the saber-toothed tiger kittens fled back into the volcano—and the Dino-Wagon swerved out of control. The Wheel Deal won the first checkpoint challenge as the remaining cars limped in behind them.

DEEP-SEA TRENCH CHECKPOI

1	Wheel Deal
2	Dino-Wagon
3	Jumping Jalopy
4	Rust Bucket 3000
5	Supersonic Sparkler
6	Flying Diaper

The stars: 6 stars for first place, 5 stars for second place, 4 stars for third place, 3 stars for fourth place, 2 stars for fifth place and 1 star for sixth place.

The checkpoint was a large entrance in the side of the trench wall. One by one, the cars moved through into a huge underwater grotto and the Wheelnuts bobbed to the surface.

The cheating Wheel Deal had won—for now. As the rest of the racers dusted themselves down, they were desperate to get their own back on the noisy and cheesy twosome. But just then, a bright-yellow sub appeared—it was Wheelie, there in person to greet the racers.

CHAPTER 8

"It's 'Wheelnut Challenge' time!" said the eccentric billionaire as he emerged from his luxury sub. "We are in an underwater grotto far below the surface. Time to stretch your legs—this will be the last fresh air you'll get before the end of the race!"

The drivers climbed out of their vehicles and onto the jetty that led into the grotto. But there wasn't going to be much time to relax as the drivers were soon seated on the water's edge.

"Now, you will already have seen some of the wonderful wildlife that is to be found in our seas," said Warren. "Well, I think it's time to get a little bit closer to some of these beautiful creatures.

just shout, 'I'm a wheelnut, get me out of here!'"

Each team sat nervously with their feet dangling in the water. There were creatures down there, but it was too murky to see exactly what they were. However, this challenge was not about *viewing* the sea life, it was all about having your toes nibbled and how long you could stand it!

The first team to get nipped was the Jumping Jalopy, and they were under attack from crustaceans!

It would make a great platter in a seafood restaurant, but not here. I'm a Wheelnut, get me out of here!

My toes are being eaten alive! Lobster, crab and crayfish!

Those fishy colors woul be great for a stage outf but ... I'm a Wheelnut, g me out of here!

The Wheel Deal had been finding this hilarious, until they too started feeling something at their feet. The flashiest, most colorful fish were nibbling away at the corny twosome's toes.

for them. Something truly shocking

The Supersonic Sparkler crew was now really worried about what was going to happen to them. Thousands of tiny fish were tickling their toes!

That *buzzz* is just not *buzzz* fair—I'm a Wheelnut, *buzzz* get me out of here!

Ha-ha! I can't take any more. I'm a ha-ha, Wheelnut, hee-hee, get me out of here!

The only teams that were finding the challenge easy were the Flying Diaper and the Dino-Wagon. With their slightly gross, smelly feet, the Flying Diaper crew were actually frightening off most of the fish.

And the feet of the Dino-Wagon duo were too leathery and thick for the sea life. Apart from the occasional very brave barracuda, they were being left alone.

It was a toss-up to see who was going to last the longest, but then a new creature appeared—one that was more than a match for the driving babies: Cleaner Shrimp! Gurgle and Burp were having their

them cheesy! I'm a Wheelnut, get me out of here!

This is like having a lovely massage!

The last team with its feet in the water was the Dino-Wagon. Wheelie simply couldn't throw in *any* creature that could take on *their* prehistoric tootsies. Turbo Rex and Flappy were not moving!

"Congratulations to the Dino-Wagon—they have been given **5 bonus Gold Stars** for winning the Challenge!" declared Wheelie. "Maybe you can spend them on some new socks! Now, Wheelnuts, back to your vehicles."

The teams were all relieved to be getting back into the safety of their submersi-cars.

CHAPTER 9

"**T**ime to return to the race," said Wheelie.
"Things are about to heat up—because the next

in to make it more interesting! Now, if you just steer
your cars into that pipe, it will transport you straight
to the Sea of Coral."

The drivers found themselves blasted along a long pipe before they were shot out one by one into a stunningly beautiful sea full of towering corals and twinkling fish. But the first hazard soon became apparent … the Jumping Jalopy had somehow sprung a leak! James and Campbell struggled frantically to stem the water pouring into their car.

As the other cars sped past, the Wheel Deal
barged the Dino-Wagon into the razor-sharp coral.

"Take that!" cackled Dustin.

"Here," said Campbell, "use these to fix the

James scrambled in the bottom of the car, frantically chewing gum and tying string around newspaper.

A moment later, he sat back up and looked hopefully at Campbell.

"That's the ticket!" Campbell laughed as the Jalopy started to rise again.

The cars in front were speeding around the course, keeping clear of the treacherous reef.

"I could stare at these gorgeous fish for hours," said Dee-Dee. "They're just like my pet fish, Fi-Fi." She dropped some fish food into Fi-Fi's tank.

"Wait a second, your pet fish has given me an idea!" said Nelly. "Remember what we bought with our last set of Gold Stars at the Wheelnut Garage?"

"The Pink Cotton-Candy-Flavored Car Freshener?" said Dee-Dee. "It smells divine …"

"No, I mean the Super Powder Splatterer. Maybe it will work underwater."

and the Flying Diaper went neck and neck with the Jumping Jalopy, they didn't realize they were right in the sights of the Supersonic Sparkler!

"FIRE!" cried Nelly. The Super Powder Splatterer began shooting out volleys of fish food. "Aim for their windshields!"

At first the other Wheelnuts weren't concerned about the thin layer of flakes that was coating their windshields, but that changed when they realized what the flakes were attracting ...

"Fish!" wailed Gurgle. "*Thousands* of them!"

Tiny tropical fish were swarming all over the Wheelnuts' windshields and they started swerving crazily all over the place! The Rust Bucket 3000 crashed into the back of the Wheel Deal … the Jumping Jalopy plunged into a sandbank and the Flying Diaper was driving upside down again *and* going in completely the wrong direction!

And among all this chaos, the Supersonic Sparkler simply cruised past the other cars and into the lead.

"See you later, losers!" chuckled Dee-Dee.

"Like taking sparkly fairy candy from a baby!" laughed Nelly. As they sped onward, they even had time to admire a large shipwreck—although it did seem slightly familiar …

"This is just going too well," said Nelly. "What could possibly go wrong?"

It was then they realized *they* were being eyed up by a hungry fish. But *this* fish wasn't interested in flakes of fish food—this fish wanted a much more substantial mouthful!

CHAPTER 10

"**H**ammerhead shark!" wailed Nelly as the huge fish lunged at the Supersonic Sparkler. "Aim the Super Powder Splatterer!"

Dee-Dee quickly reloaded the Splatterer, aimed and fired—but the shark kept on heading right at them.

Dee-Dee kept on firing, but the scowling Hammerhead was closing in faster and faster ...

"I've tried tickling dust, sneezing powder and liquid itch, but nothing works!" panicked Dee-Dee.

The shark was getting closer and closer and the
other Wheelnuts were soon aware of it—the little

atoll—the shark was going to
them off one by one ...

But just when all seemed lost, the shark
suddenly turned tail and swam away—*crying!*

It didn't take long for the Wheelnuts to work out why the shark had left in such as hurry … a creature far, far bigger loomed over them. And just like the shark, it had its mouth wide open, but this mouth was HUGE! James was the first driver to recognize what the creature was.

"It's a blue whale!" he said. "They eat microscopic krill—it won't be interested in us!"

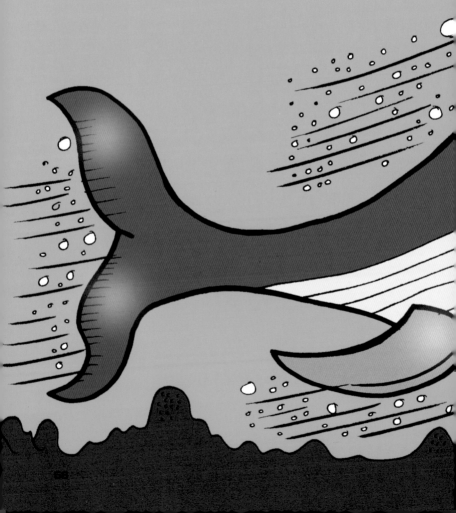

But their joy was short-lived because if blue whales were supposed to live on krill, no one had ~~~~~~~th and lunged

The blue whale had swallowed every last Wheelnut and with a flick of its mighty tail swam off into the murky depths. But the silence of the ocean was disturbed by a cackling laugh coming from the shipwreck.

"Getting that whale to swallow a brain-control device was a stroke of genius!" said Dipstick proudly.

"I can manipulate the whale's every move!" said Wipeout, patting the remote control. "My brother's bothersome race gone in a gulp. Big, blue and beautifully evil!"

CACKLE! CACKLE! CACKLE!

pile of g̶r̶...
One by one, the drivers c̶...

"Step into the spotlight!" said Dustin as he lit up the Wheel Deal's huge light.

"Turn that thing off!" wailed Myley. "My stage outfit is all slimy and my hair is seriously malfunctioning."

"There's no time to worry about what you look like," said Campbell as he wrung slime out of his moustache. "We need to get out of here!"

Something started beeping on the Rust Bucket 3000. "My sensors are picking up a metallic object," said Boltz. "Whales aren't made out of metal—the metallic object *has* to be responsible for its strange behavior."

Sure enough, wedged out of reach at the top of the whale's tummy, was a small metal box. It was beeping and had a small red light on it.

"A remote control device!" said Nutz. "We've got to bring that thing down!"

...y would a blue whale have a remote
...? And who would *do* such a
...d asked the

...

"It's time to ge...
that nasty race wrecker!" said ...

James volunteered for the task of tickling the whale's tonsils—but the other drivers would have to get him up there.

James stood in position on the Dino-Wagon's volcano.

Flappy pushed the volcano to "full power." Just as it felt like the car would blow up, it released a huge gust of smoke and James flew upward!

WHUFF!

The Flying Diaper then unleashed their second

He then had only a fraction of a second to use one of Dee-Dee's pink dusters to tickle the tonsils.

Then he plummeted downward towards Myley and Dustin who were there to catch him on a stretched-out stage outfit.

At first the Whale just cleared his throat. James had definitely tickled it in the right place. Then with an almighty ocean-shaking splutter, it coughed the Wheelnuts out high into the sky above the sea and with them the remote-control device!

"Wheeee!" screeched Burp as the Flying Diaper flew through the air.

"At least we should have a soft landing!" said Dee-Dee as the Supersonic Sparkler started to plummet back towards the sea.

"Hold tiiiiiiiiiiiight!" screeched Flappy as they zoomed closer and closer to the water.

CHAPTER 12

One by one the cars splashed into the sea and it

"I don't think we need to do anything," chuckled Campbell. "I think there's an angry whale who is doing that for us!"

In the distance, a shipwreck-shaped sub was going at top speed as the huge angry blue whale chased it off.

Now that Wipeout was off the scene, the cars could finally concentrate on racing, and with a big blue empty ocean, it was time for the drivers to really use their skills. The Dino-Wagon was zooming through the water thanks to its new volcanic rock powering its engine, but the Rust Bucket 3000 was right behind them.

"Computer says we need more power!" said Nutz.

"*We've* got all the power we need!" cackled Turbo Rex.

The Supersonic Sparkler was also getting a rhythm going and they were in close pursuit of the Flying Diaper and the Wheel Deal.

The next checkpoint was now in sight and the gold stars were still anyone's to win. Anyone apart from the Jumping Jalopy—they were falling farther

"Or a shoal of fish," said Campbell.

"But there are no fish out here," said James as he looked at the vast open ocean around them.

"There are fish out here all right," said Campbell. "You just need to know how to attract them. Steer the car up to the surface. It's time to put our Wheelnut Garage upgrade to the test …"

James couldn't see how their upgrade could help, but given that they were in last place, it had to be worth a try. The car was now racing along on top of the water, and beneath them the other racers were shooting towards the checkpoint.

"Now what, Grandpa?" said James. "I can't see any fish …"

"Set the superfast propeller to top speed—I want to create as much disturbance as possible!" said Campbell.

The water began to churn and froth … but there was nothing. Then James noticed a large dark shadow under the water.

"Tuna!" said Campbell. "The disturbance on the surface has made them think there is a shoal of small fish to feed on … now, head for the

checkpoint, the Jumping Jalopy just needed to cruise beneath the surface to take first place. As the rest of the Wheelnuts passed through, checkpoint Gold Stars were allocated …

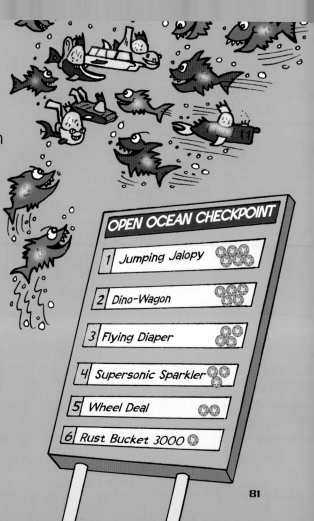

OPEN OCEAN CHECKPOINT

1	Jumping Jalopy	⭐⭐⭐⭐⭐⭐
2	Dino-Wagon	⭐⭐⭐⭐⭐
3	Flying Diaper	⭐⭐⭐⭐
4	Supersonic Sparkler	⭐⭐⭐
5	Wheel Deal	⭐⭐
6	Rust Bucket 3000	⭐

CHAPTER 13

With the final checkpoint passed, it was now a race to the finish. But as with all Wheelnuts races, Warren "Wheelie" Wheelnut was not going to make it easy and he had a few final salty surprises in store for the racers. Having seen fish and sea life of every shape and size, what was about to happen next took them all completely by surprise …

WI

The course now led the cars through an area
filled with large, sinister-looking metal objects.

"Mines!" said Campbell. "Touch one of those

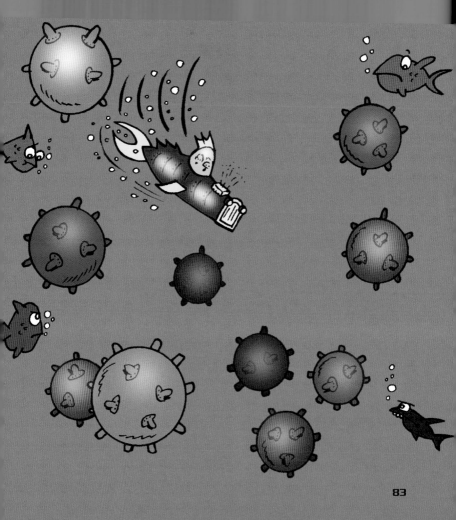

The Wheelnuts started to drive nervously through the minefield. And it wasn't long before they were discovering the "surprises" the mines contained—they were raining down brightly colored squid ink and tickly seaweed!

It was almost impossible to drive on as huge clouds of colorful ink blocked the route and seaweed clung to the sides of the cars …

The cars finally emerged from the minefield and they were hard to recognize!

"I always wondered what the car would look like in purple," said Campbell.

"I think pink looks quite nice," said Burp.

But there was no time to admire the cars' new paint as the finish line loomed up ahead!

The cars were now entering the final phase of the race in a sprint to the finish—but the Wheelnuts *just* had time for some final cheats!

As the Dino-Wagon wrestled for first place with the Rust Bucket 3000, suddenly the racers noticed something ahead that made them all stop in their tracks. There were two bits of wildlife, the likes of

these frighteningly fluffy creatures.

But all of a sudden one of the cars sped past—they weren't scared of the teddies at all. The Flying Diaper cackled with laughter.

"I knew those giant teddy bears would come in handy!" chortled Burp. "The best Wheelnut Garage buy *ever!*"

"They're petrified of them!" snorted Gurgle. "I can almost *smell* the checkered flag!"

CHAPTER 14

As soon as the Flying Diaper shot past, the other drivers realized they had been tricked. There

when they started going backward!

"You're not the only ones to buy a cheat from the Wheelnut Garage!" said Nutz. "Now, reel 'em in!"

The Rust Bucket 3000 had a brand-new fishing rod attachment and Boltz reeled in the Flying Diaper. The Rust Bucket 3000 scooped first place, winning the race!

The cars all floated to the surface and drove back onto solid ground. The first three cars were in position to receive their trophies.

"You may be wet, Wheelnuts, but congratulations to you all!" said Wheelie as he handed out trophies to the top three cars.

"In third place, we have the Wheel Deal—you get the Jellyfish Medal.

"In second place is the Dino-Wagon, you get the Coral Cup ...

and in first place, receiving the Terrifying Tuna Trophy ... it's the Rust Bucket 3000!!"

Final Race Placings

3 | Wheel Deal

4 | Flying Diaper

5 | Jumping Jalopy

6 | Supersonic Sparkler

The drivers were really relieved to be able to dry off. And then all of a sudden there was a rumbling noise … something was about to blow on the back of the Dino-Wagon.

"The volcanic rock—it seems to be unstable!" wailed Flappy.

"LOOK OUT!!!" screeched Turbo Rex. The drivers only just had time to duck as the back of the Dino-Wagon blew off!

"Looks like you'll be spending your Gold Stars on a new volcano!" chuckled Wheelie. "Well,

Champion after the final race!

"I can't wait to spend, spend, spend!" said Campbell. "A gold gear stick, a turbo exhaust … and a new soccer ball for you, James!"

"Well, whatever you buy, make sure you join us for Race 5 in the Craziest Race on Earth!" said Warren.

Turn over for a sneak peek of the next course …